Fairy Magic

COLORING BOOK

GWYMBELL TRACY
C O L O R I N G   B O O K S

Have questions? Let us know.
gwymbelltracy@gmail.com

www.ingramcontent.com/pod-product-compliance
Lightning Source LLC
Chambersburg PA
CBHW081955210726
48294CB00014B/2042